J Taddon
Taddonio, Lea
The Deadwood Hill trap

$28.50
on1005308127

BY LEA TADDONIO   ILLUSTRATED BY ALESSIA TRUNFIO

LUCKY 8

#4 The Deadwood Hill Trap

Spellbound

An Imprint of Magic Wagon
abdopublishing.com

To Jarah, Bronte and Poppy – LT

To my Family, my Love, my best friends and Eva. Thank you all
for helping me to make it real in all your personal ways. – AT

abdopublishing.com

Published by Magic Wagon, a division of ABDO, PO Box 398166,
Minneapolis, Minnesota 55439. Copyright © 2018 by Abdo Consulting
Group, Inc. International copyrights reserved in all countries. No
part of this book may be reproduced in any form without written
permission from the publisher. Spellbound™ is a trademark and logo
of Magic Wagon.

Printed in the United States of America, North Mankato, Minnesota.
092017
012018

**THIS BOOK CONTAINS
RECYCLED MATERIALS**

Written by Lea Taddonio
Illustrated by Alessia Trunfio
Edited by Heidi M.D. Elston
Art Directed by Laura Mitchell

Publisher's Cataloging-in-Publication Data

Names: Taddonio, Lea, author. | Trunfio, Alessia, illustrator.
Title: The Deadwood Hill trap / by Lea Taddonio; illustrated by Alessia Trunfio.
Description: Minneapolis, Minnesota : Magic Wagon, 2018. | Series: Lucky 8; Book 4
Summary: Makayla and Liam enter the Topsy-Turvy, only to discover Jo Ann George
    tricked them. Will they be stuck there forever?
Identifiers: LCCN 2017946547 | ISBN 9781532130564 (lib.bdg.) | ISBN 9781532131165 (ebook) |
    ISBN 9781532131462 (Read-to-me ebook)
Subjects: LCSH: Science fiction–Juvenile fiction. | Ghosts–Juvenile fiction. | Good and
    evil–Juvenile fiction. | Brothers and sisters–Juvenile fiction.
Classification: DDC [FIC]–dc23
LC record available at https://lccn.loc.gov/2017946547

TABLE OF CONTENTS

CHAPTER #1
The Topsy-Turvy 4

CHAPTER #2
A Trick 16

CHAPTER #3
Jo Ann's Plan 29

CHAPTER #4
Safe at Home. 42

The Topsy-Turvy

I fall through empty space
and hit the ground hard. Pain
EXPLODES through
my hands and knees. There is
a **CRASH** and a sharp yelp
beside me.

"Makayla?" My brother, Liam's, voice is so quiet, barely a breath. "Makayla, are you there?"

"Yes," I whisper in the same low tone. I rub my eyes and then **BLINK**. "Can you see anything? Anything at all?" My sight is gone. The world is **BLACK**.

"Nothing." Liam sounds more worried. "I'm totally **BLIND**."

I feel around the ground beneath my hands. The little **STONES** are damp and cool to the touch. The air is *frosty* as an autumn morning.

Only one minute ago, we were

sitting outside my bedroom window.

In the **WITCH'S** tree.

Our new house, Deadwood Hill, has
a **_MYSTERY_**. A girl who used to
live there went **MISSING**. A girl
named Jo Ann George. Now she's in
this place she calls the Topsy-Turvy.

We've come to try and **RESCUE** her.

I spread out my arms. They hit

rock walls. "We're in a tunnel,"

I say. "Let's start crawling."

"How do you know the way out?"

my brother asks worriedly.

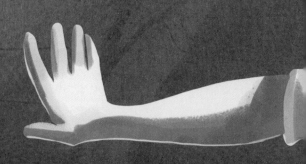

"I don't." I **ROLL** my eyes.

I guess it's good he can't see my

face. "Do you have a better idea?"

He's quiet a minute. Our breath

sounds loud. My heartbeat **POUNDS**

so hard I can hear it in my ears.

"Then let's move," I *HISS*. "You don't want to stay here, do you?"

Chapter 2

A Trick

A tiny light appears

in the distance. We keep

crawling. The light grows

STRONGER

and brighter. At last we're

at the end of the TUNNEL.

We can stand.

Liam and I look around. It appears we're inside a **CAVE**. It's almost as big as our high school gym. *Fireflies* flit back and forth, casting a strange light.

"Hello?" I call, taking a step

FORWARD. "Jo Ann?

Are you there? Can you hear me?"

No one answers.

"Shhhh!" My brother tugs
my hand. "Are you CRAZY?
What if you wake up whoever—or
whatever—is hiding down there?"

He points at a dark pool
of water *swirling* like a
whirlpool. Beside it lays a large
stick. The wood is pure white.

"Hey, that looks like it came from the **WITCH'S** tree," I say, walking over.

"Wait, **STOP**! Don't touch anything," my brother calls. But I ignore him. I lift the stick in the air.

"That's how I contacted you."

We turn toward the voice coming

from the **SHADOWS**.

"I put that stick in the water

and **TRACED** the words

that you both read."

I frown. "That we read where?"

"Why, the Magic 8 Ball, of course." A young girl steps into the *firefly* light. She wiggles her fingers in a small wave and winks.

I gasp, recognizing her face from the newspapers. "Jo Ann George!" I cry. But she doesn't look relieved we have come to RESCUE her. Instead she looks as if she knows a secret joke.

She gives a nasty giggle. "I can't believe you fell for my little trick."

Chapter 3

Jo Ann's Plan

"What do you mean? We're
here to rescue you," I say.
My throat is TIGHT. I don't
understand what is happening. But
something feels WRONG.

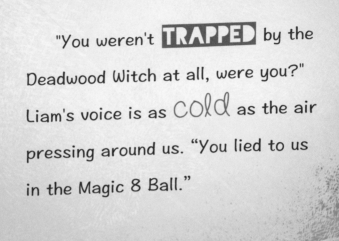

"You weren't **TRAPPED** by the Deadwood Witch at all, were you?" Liam's voice is as cold as the air pressing around us. "You lied to us in the Magic 8 Ball."

"You lied! Boo-hoo!" Jo Ann's
cruel laugh echoes across the cave.

"Hah, you are both idiots!" she **SNARLS**. "I wasn't trapped by the Deadwood Witch. I *am* the Deadwood Witch. Reborn."

I can't even **GASP**. My mouth is dry.

"When my mother wanted to punish me, she'd make me pull WEEDS in the garden. That's how I discovered the witch's old spell book. It was buried in a **flower** bed beneath the tree where she was hung."

Liam and I take a step back. But there is **NOWHERE** to go. No escape.

"My parents didn't understand. I'm meant for great things! So I cast a spell from the book." Her smile holds no humor. "A disappearing spell."

"That's terrible!" Liam shouts. "You're a MONSTER!"

"But I did something wrong." Jo Ann's lips flatten in a thin line. "My parents didn't disappear. I did."

"Now I'm TRAPPED here. In this place." She looks around. "The Topsy-Turvy. But I've learned I can leave . . . if I find someone to take my place."

"Us," I say. The blood **drains** from my face.

"Thank you for volunteering," she sneers.

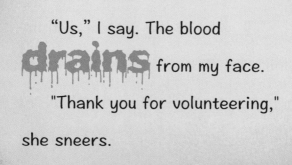

"I'll swim to the bottom of this whirlpool. Then **magic** will take me back to the real world. You'll be the ones **STUCK** here. You'll be left writing messages in the Magic 8 Ball."

She turns with a laugh, ready to
dive into the black water. CRACK!
Liam holds the white stick as Jo
Ann SlumpS to the ground.

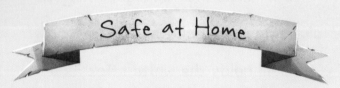

CHAPTER 4

Safe at Home

"It's okay," he says before I can scream. "Jo Ann is still breathing. But she'll have a **nasty** headache."

"Good." My face is grim. "She tricked us. She tried to trap us here forever."

Jo Ann stirs on the ground. A **MOAN** escapes her lips.

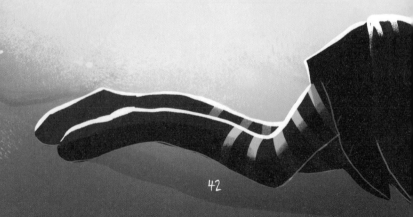

43

"Let's go," Liam says. "Before she wakes up."

We dive into the *whirlpool*. The water is dark as night and feels slimy on my skin. The DEEPER we swim, the more the water churns. It's like going through a washing machine.

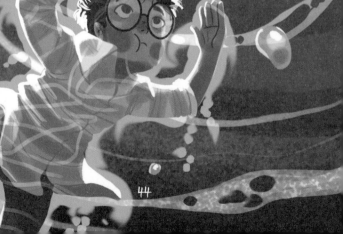

POP!

Faster than a **BLINK**, we are back in our yard beneath the Deadwood tree.

The sun is out. Birds are *singing*.

"Are you okay?" I turn, grabbing my brother's hand.

"It's GONE." He looks around. His face worried. "We had the Magic 8 Ball before we went into the Topsy-Turvy. Now it's GONE."

We look at each other with scared faces. We got *lucky*. We are safe. But this wasn't a dream.

Jo Ann George is still trapped in the Topsy-Turvy. She is waiting. And someday she will try to turn someone else's life into a waking NIGHTMARE.

48